Koala
and the
Flower

Mary Murphy

EGMONT CHILDREN'S BOOKS

Badger and Raccoon see things in black and white. They are always sure that they are always right. Little grey Koala isn't sure about many things. She asks lots of questions.

Badger knows that Badger is right.

Raccoon knows that Raccoon is right.

And they

both know

that they know

much more than Koala.

One day, Koala goes for a walk.

She goes slowly, looking at things from all sides.

She finds something new. It is a yellow flower.

Koala has never

seen a yellow

flower before,

except in a picture.

Koala runs all the way home…

"Guess what I saw!" she says.
"A yellow flower! Come and see!"

But Badger and Raccoon are too busy.

Koala picks the flower
and brings it home.

"**Where** do flowers come from?" she asks.

Badger and Raccoon are sure they know.

Koala puts the flower in a jar so that she can look at it.

She doesn't know that flowers need water.

The flower dies.

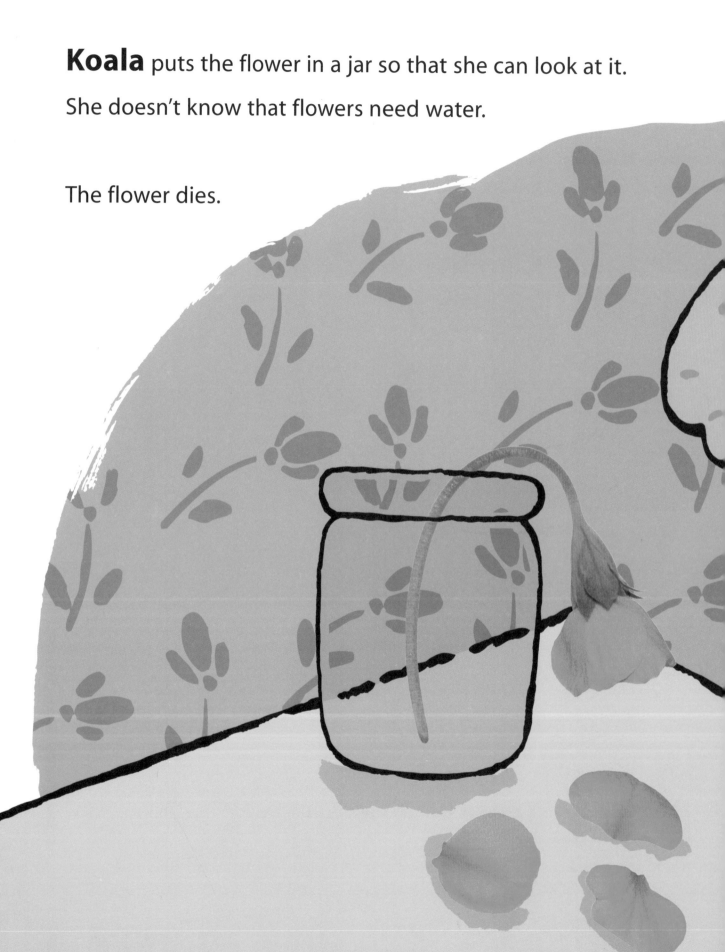

"Poor flower!" says Koala.

"I should have left you where you were."

MAKING FLOWERS (by Raccoon)

1.

Raccoon shows Koala
how to make flowers.

2.

They fetch paper and wire
and string and glue.

3.

They cut and twist
and tie and stick.

4.

But it doesn't turn out right.
"You did it wrong," says Raccoon.

MAKING FLOWERS (by Badger)

Badger shows Koala
how to make flowers.

They fetch flour and milk
and sugar and butter.

They sift and stir
and roll and bake.

But it doesn't turn out right.
"You did it wrong," says Badger.

Koala goes for another walk with some flower biscuits in her backpack.

She walks and walks and walks. She goes further than she

...as ever gone before.

She meets a little grey donkey. (He looks very big to Koala.) Koala tells him about her flower.

"I don't know how to make flowers," says Donkey.

"But there is a place I go when I want to find out things."

Koala didn't know there were so many books in the world. She didn't know there were so many animals trying to find out things. She didn't know that most animals know that they don't know everything.

"This is great!" she says.

Koala goes home with a backpack full of books.

She reads…

…and reads.

Koala buys some seeds.

"Now I can make some flowers," she says.

She shakes seeds from her own beloved flower too.

Badger and Raccoon snigger. They laugh when she digs a patch in a sunny part of the garden.

They guffaw when she puts the seeds on the ground and covers them with earth.

They roll about when she sprinkles water on the seeds. But Koala doesn't care.

Koala reads her library books and waits for her seeds to grow. Sometimes the sun shines…

And sometimes clouds bring rain.

After a few days, little green spikes poke out of the earth. Koala tends the flower patch. She carries snails away.

She waters the earth. Soon little buds appear on top of the little green spikes. Time goes by and…

…this is what happens.

"Come and see!" says Koala to Badger and Raccoon.

"Well done!" says Badger. "Just what I expected."

"Me too!" says Raccoon. "First rate!"

"I knew it!" says Koala. "I knew it would work!"

Now Koala knows about lots of flowers, and insects, and colours.

"It's still like magic," she says…

Thank you, Koala!

"…at least that's what I think!"